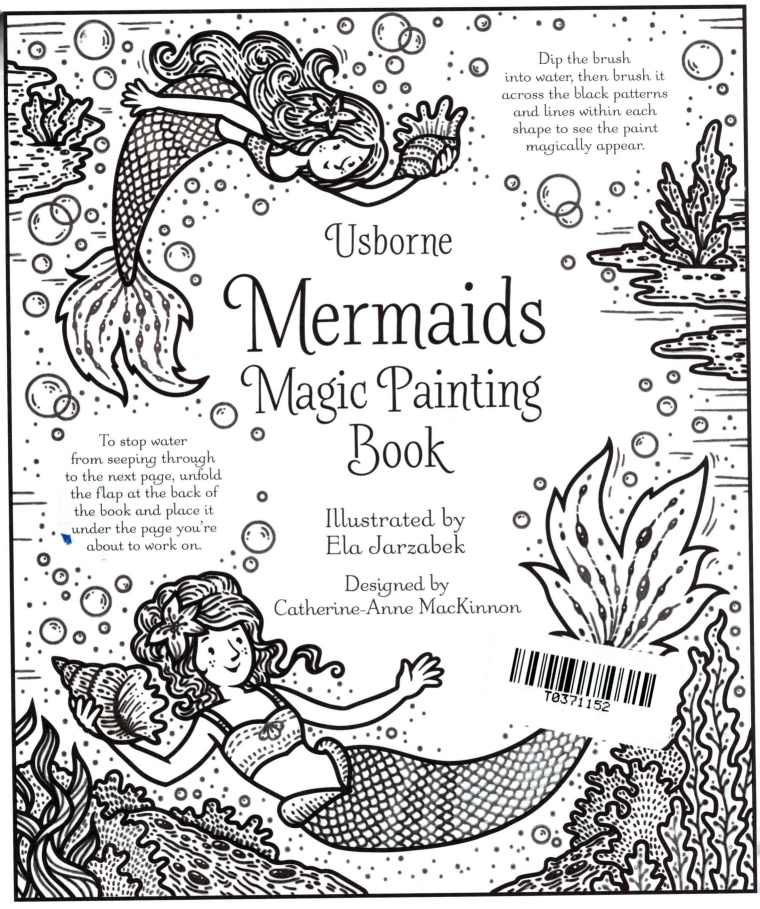

Dip the brush into water, then brush it across the black patterns and lines within each shape to see the paint magically appear.

Usborne
Mermaids
Magic Painting
Book

To stop water from seeping through to the next page, unfold the flap at the back of the book and place it under the page you're about to work on.

Illustrated by
Ela Jarzabek

Designed by
Catherine-Anne MacKinnon